TOM FEELINGS

I SAW YOUR FACE

TEXT BY **KWAME DAWES**
AFTERWORD BY **JERRY PINKNEY**

DIAL BOOKS  *NEW YORK*

For
Lorna,
Sena, Kekeli, and Akua,
Mama the Great
and the Tribe:
Gwyneth, Kojo, Aba, Adjoa, Kojovi
—K.D.

Published by Dial Books
A member of Penguin Group (USA) Inc.
345 Hudson Street • New York, New York 10014

Text copyright © 2005 by Kwame Dawes
Art copyright © 2005 by The Estate of Tom Feelings
Map illustration copyright © 2005 by Christopher Calderhead
Afterword copyright © 2005 by Jerry Pinkney, used with permission
All rights reserved • Designed by Nancy R. Leo-Kelly
Text set in Elan • Manufactured in China on acid-free paper
1 3 5 7 9 10 8 6 4 2

Library of Congress Cataloging-in-Publication Data
Dawes, Kwame Senu Neville, date.
I saw your face / [drawings by] Tom Feelings ; text by Kwame Dawes.
p.   cm.
Summary: A poem and portraits of children illustrate the shared beauty and heritage of
people of African descent living throughout the world.
ISBN 0-8037-1894-2
1. Africa—Emigration and immigration—Juvenile poetry. 2. Africans—Foreign countries—Juvenile poetry. 3. Children's poetry, Jamaican.
4. Africa—Juvenile poetry. [1. Blacks—Poetry. 2. Face—Poetry. 3. Caribbean poetry (English).] I. Feelings, Tom. II. Title.
PR9265.9.D39115 2005   811'.54—dc22

INTRODUCTION

My mother, who is Ghanaian, is an artist. She has traveled a great deal and she has developed this little game that she likes to play. When she meets people of West African descent, she tries to place them in a West African ethnic group. She is quite good at this. Despite the years of migration and cultural mixing, she is still able to identify ethnic characteristics in Africans living in Europe, the Americas, and Asia. It is her face game. With each identification she is telling a story that is old and rich with the truth of survival despite suffering. I too have traveled much between Africa, the Caribbean, Canada, and where I live now in South Carolina. And in all my travels I have had this peculiar sense of seeing faces that look so familiar even though I could never have seen those faces before.

One day, Tom Feelings and I were talking about his journeys around the world and he told me about all the faces that he saw in Africa that he had seen in New York, where he grew up, and in Guyana, where he worked for years, and in the many places he had visited around the world where people of African descent live. He commented about the rich history of African people, a history that is told through the multiplication of faces. We both recognized something beautiful and meaningful in what we were discovering.

Tom gave me a large folder full of drawings he had done all over the world, and apart from the sheer beauty of these faces, the wonderful grace in the faces of these young people, I saw a story of resilience and pride in the faces. This was the story of Africa and her diaspora.

Peter Tosh, a Jamaican reggae musician, used to sing a song that still holds true today: "Don't care where you come from, as long as you're a black man, you're an African." I wrote the poem "I Saw Your Face" as a response to Tom's wonderful drawings. I imagined the many stories and connections in all these faces and I decided to take a journey with them through the many worlds that have become home for people of African descent: the cities, the cold streets, the savannahs, the favelas, the hill country, the beach villages, and every other place where African people live. It means something that we recognize our shared beauty and our shared heritage.

Tom and I had a wonderful time telling stories and enjoying the pleasures of such a rich collaboration, and playing, in our own way, my mother's little game. In many ways, we saw the whole project come to full fruition in the splendid handmade booklets that he does before even thinking of publication. He loved the poem and was generous enough to make these lines sit side by side with his marvelous art.

This book is lasting testament to Tom's kindness and visionary force. I hope you too will cherish the work as much as I do.

Kwame Dawes

I saw your face in Benin
And in Ghana near Takoradi.
Then there on the plains of Bahia
Your gentle eyes said hi.

I saw that face in Kingston
Under a green cocoa tree
And when I stopped at a Castries market
Those same eyes welcomed me.

Cruising through Louisiana
Past a field of collard greens
There you were in your overalls
Your eyes still following me.

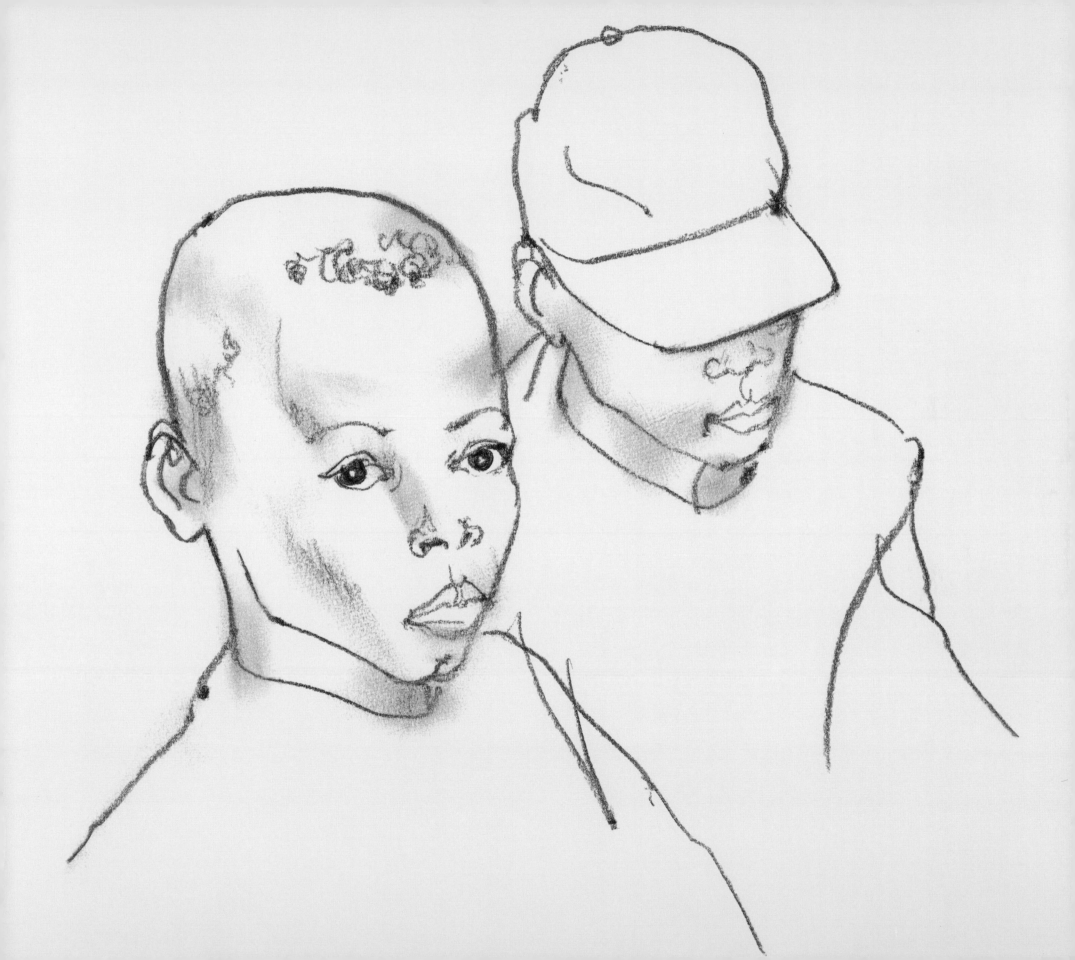

I saw you waiting for the Brixton bus
Late January in London Town.
You closed your eyes and quietly dreamed
Of sand, sea grapes, and sun.

On the porch of a slanting old house
On a street in New Orleans

I saw you there with your turned-up hair
And your golden looped earrings.

I saw you deep in thought
While waves crashed ashore in Suriname.

Were you thinking those same thoughts
When you gazed at me in Birmingham?

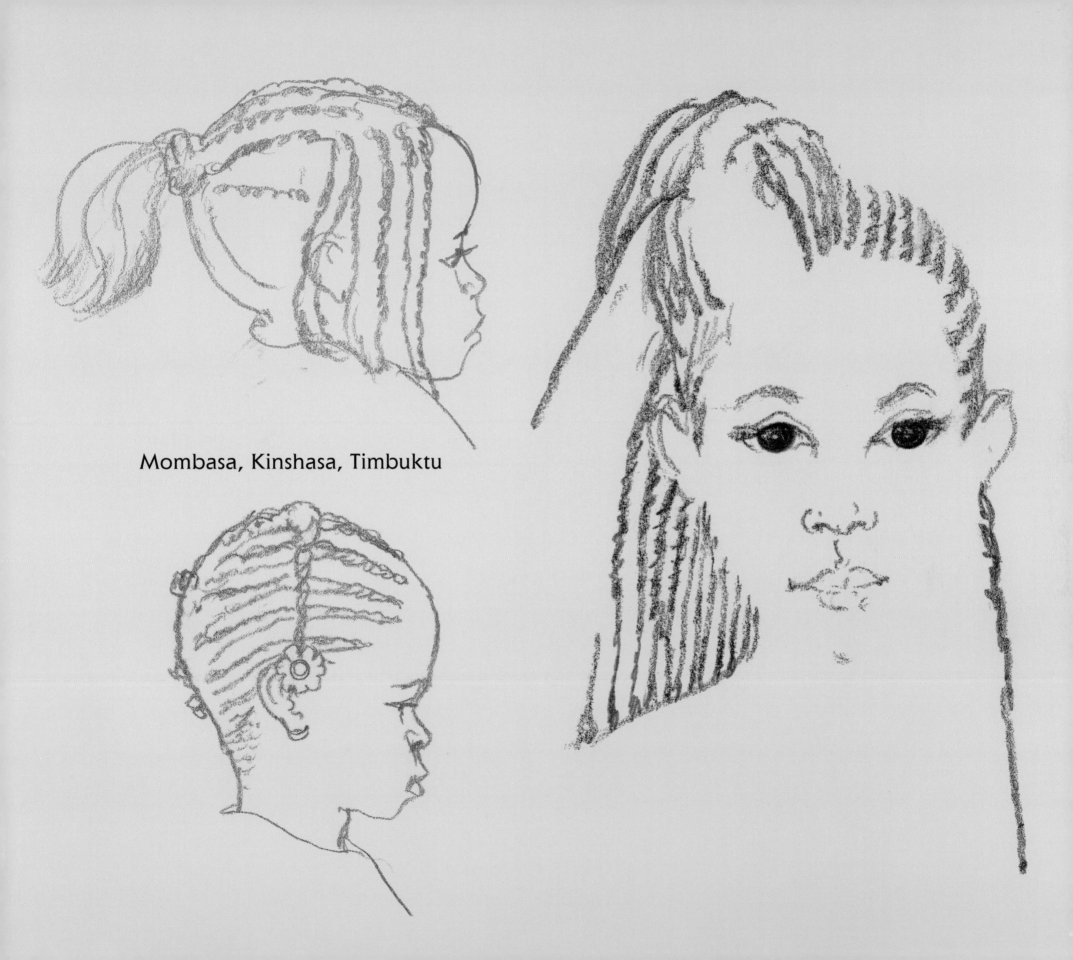

Mombasa, Kinshasa, Timbuktu

Havana, Savannah, Port-au-Prince

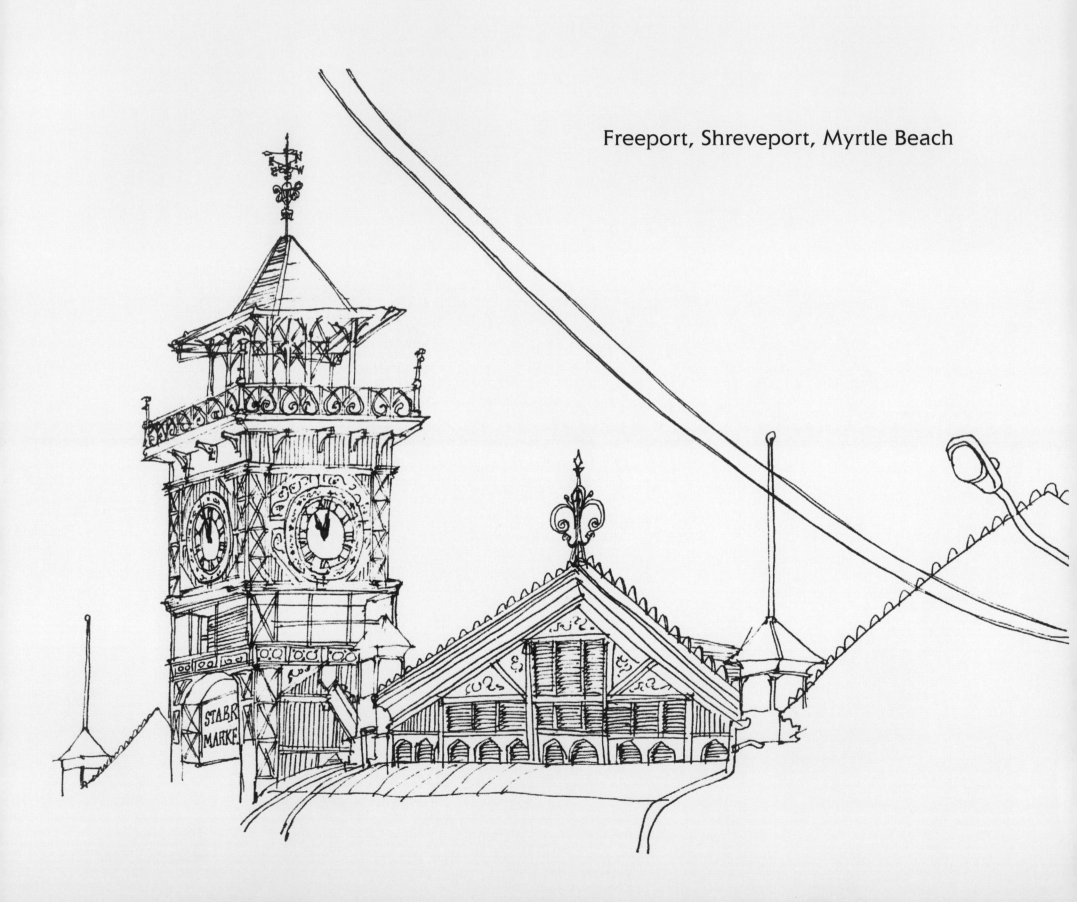

Freeport, Shreveport, Myrtle Beach

Lomé, Lagos, Abidjan

Everywhere I turn I see you there
In the flat wetlands and on windswept coasts.

I see your face look back at me
Full of ancient stories and dreams

That tell me we have traveled far
And survived the journeys well.

NORTH AMERICA

ATLANTIC

TEXAS

LOUISIANA

ALABAMA

GEORGIA

SOUTH CAROLINA

CUBA

HAITI

JAMAICA

CASTRIES
Saint Lucia

SURINAME

SOUTH AMERICA

BRAZIL

STATE OF
BAHIA

TEXAS

SHREVEPORT

LOUISIANA

FREEPORT

NEW ORLEANS

BIRMINGHAM

ALABAMA

GEORGIA

SOUTH CAROLINA

MYRTLE BEACH

SAVANNAH

HAVANA

CUBA

PORT-AU-
PRINCE
HAITI

KINGSTON
JAMAICA

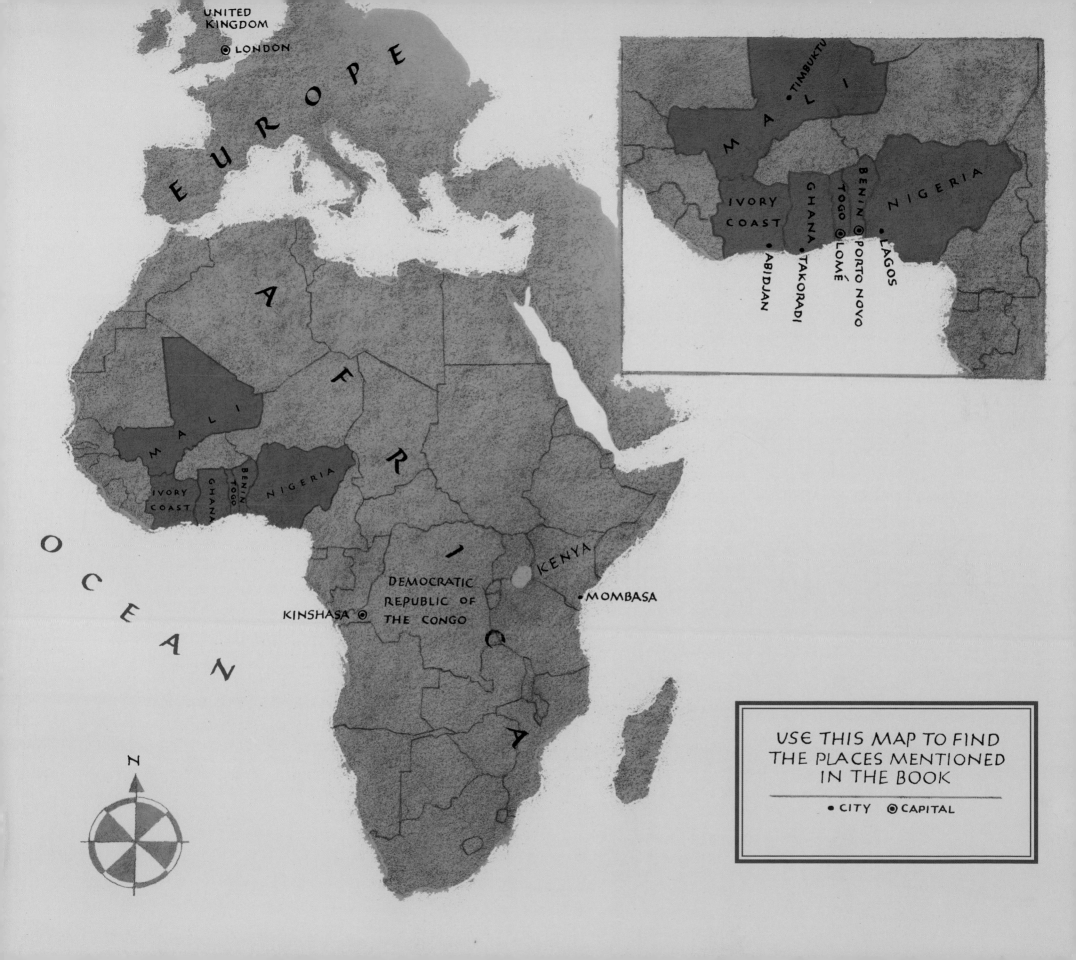

EUROPE

UNITED
KINGDOM
◎ LONDON

M A L I

TIMBUKTU

IVORY
COAST

GHANA

BENIN
TOGO

NIGERIA

PORTO NOVO
◎ LOMÉ

LAGOS

ABIDJAN

TAKORADI

AFRICA

OCEAN

IVORY
COAST

GHANA

BENIN
TOGO

NIGERIA

M
A
L
I

KENYA

DEMOCRATIC
REPUBLIC OF
THE CONGO

KINSHASA ◎

MOMBASA

N

USE THIS MAP TO FIND
THE PLACES MENTIONED
IN THE BOOK

• CITY   ◎ CAPITAL

IN MEMORY OF TOM FEELINGS

My FIRST MEETING WITH TOM FEELINGS is elusive. I have been trying to recall when he and I met in person. It was likely at a literature conference or possibly at an art exhibition and reception during the early 1980s. Even before that, however, the moment when I first viewed Tom's work, there was an overwhelming sense that I knew something about the man. One could say, my first meeting with Tom came at the moment I held a copy of *To Be a Slave* by Julius Lester, and marveled at Tom's finely crafted illustrations. I would get to know Tom more intimately through his lyrical paintings trying their best to spring from the pages of *Moja Means One,* and then *Jambo Means Hello*.

I do remember spending time with Tom at a celebration of children's literature, some years ago in Miami, Florida. We shared lunch and spirited conversation. Later we participated on a panel, where the topic was *The Role of the Black Artist in Literature.* When I listen to the tape cassette of that discussion, I am reminded of just how dedicated and passionate he was about his work, and how clearly he articulated his role as artist. One of the things he said that struck me was, "As a black artist, what I want to do is bring something new to any form that I work with. Personally, I have to work at bringing black consciousness to whatever I do." And that he did.

Through his art Tom Feelings had the ability, as with other out-standing artists such as John Biggers and Charles White, to lift our sense of self and to enable us to be in touch with our humanness, thereby making us more alert to the world we all share. For Tom, it was imperative to make art and to have his art speak to his heritage, a heritage of the uniqueness of the people of Africa and African descent.

This book *I Saw Your Face* demonstrates the wide range his life and his art spanned. I think of Tom as a visual journalist, a recorder of the worlds he traveled, from Kingston to Benin, from Ghana to Louisiana. His pictures bring us face-to-face with diverse people as we stroll past a Castries market or a slanting old house in New Orleans.

How is it that art created with such expressively nuanced line, paintings on board and ever so fragile tissue paper, could hold so much power? Or that black-and-white drawings, and paintings, could seem so rich in color? His drawings are so well crafted that at first glance, one is not aware of the line, but is led directly into the humanity of his subjects. Tom created art from the heart. His works portray passionate conviction and unflinching honesty, and his linear technique carries the message. His art reaches out and touches us in a manner that compels us to partner in his vision of the beauty and rhythm of black life. Tom embraced life and expressed it in his art. We now hold, in our hands, that gift.

Jerry Pinkney